Dear Same Josh
Enjoy!
Judy ☺

Last Night I Had a
Laughmare

Bedtime Adventures in Gigglyville

by

J.E. Laufer

Illustrated by

Jeff Yesh

GIGGLYVILLE

Published by
LITTLE EGG PUBLISHING COMPANY
PHOENIX, ARIZONA

www.LittleEggPublishing.com

www.LaughmareBook.com

Library of Congress Cataloging-in-Publication Data

Laufer, Judy Egett.
    Last night I had a laughmare : bedtime adventures in Gigglyville / by J.E. Laufer ; illustrated by Jeff Yesh.

    p. : col. ill. ; cm.

    Summary: In the magical world of Gigglyville, you will see star-hung swings, purple hair, shoelaces made of spaghetti, just to name a few! A magical bedtime rhyming story for sleepyheads of all ages, taking them on an exciting romp through the land of Gigglyville.
    Interest age group: 003-007.
    ISBN: 978-1-881669-01-2

    1. Imaginary places--Juvenile fiction. 2. Dreams--Juvenile fiction. 3. Bedtime--Juvenile fiction. 4. Imaginary places--Fiction. 5. Dreams--Fiction. 6. Bedtime--Fiction. 7. Stories in rhyme. I. Yesh, Jeff, 1971- II. Title.

PZ8.3.L346 Las 2012
[E]   2012905827

Printed in the United States of America

Produced by Five Star Publications, Inc.
Illustrator: Jeff Yesh
Editor: Jennifer Steele Christensen
Cover & Page Layout: Kris Taft Miller
Project Manager: Patti Crane
Publishing Consultant: Linda F. Radke

Photographer: Kelley Kruke Photography

Text is printed on 10% PCW stock

This book belongs to:

For—
My ever smiling dad, who made me laugh every day.
I know he would have loved this book!

My darling mom, who is so proud of all I do.

My wonderful son Andrew, the "one and only."

My soul mate and husband Nathan, who discovered my
"Laughmare" one morning.

For my family and good friends, who continue to cheer me on!

Note to the Reader:

This book is about adventure, laughter, and imagination! I wrote it to help parents and
children everywhere enjoy and look forward to sharing a funny story at bedtime.

Children, please come visit Gigglyville often. I created it for you!
Bring your parents along, too. Laughing out loud is good for sleepyheads of all ages.

I hope reading my story helps you have a happier night's sleep.
Who knows? You may wake up to a happier morning, too!

- J.E. Laufer

...until you **scream.**

5

It's about silly names and upside-down **places**;

Tying your shoes with spaghetti instead of with **laces**.

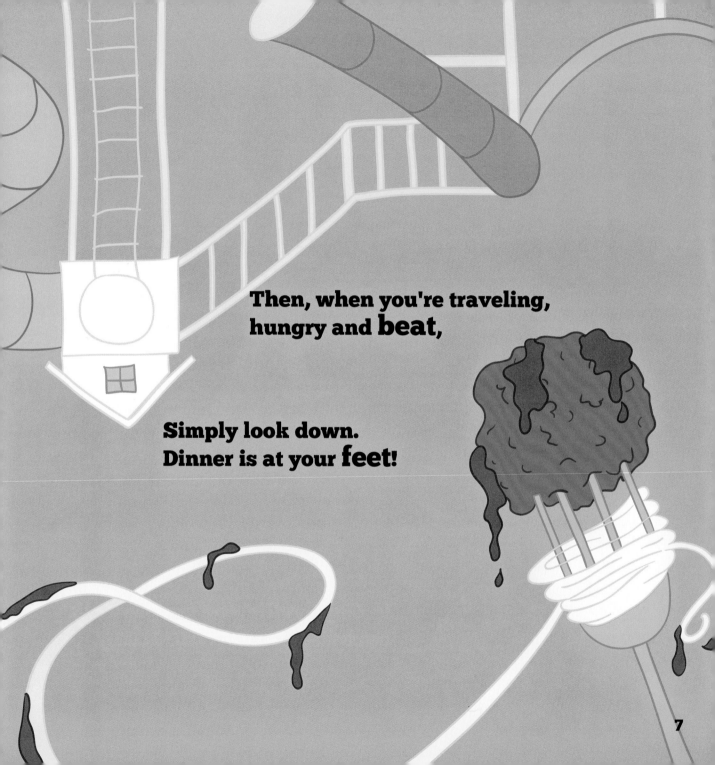

Then, when you're traveling, hungry and **beat**,

Simply look down.
Dinner is at your **feet!**

In Gigglyville, the people walk backwards when **meeting**.

Instead of "Hello",
"Good-bye" is their **greeting.**

They have unusual names, and they can grant special **wishes**—

Meet Liverlips, Smellyfeet, PurplePudding and **Dishes!**

They can turn your hair purple,
make your food taste like **candy**;

All their magical powers can
come in quite **handy!**

When you first look at them,
you may think they are **silly**,

Especially Onion Breath,
Loopy or little **Willy**.

Their clothes are ridiculous,
either too huge or too **small**,

And their height can change
daily, from tiny to **tall**.

16

Their snowballs are ice cream,
their rain tastes like **honey**—

It gets kind of sticky, but
they think it's **funny!**

Gigglyville is a land where all the numbers run **free**.

Would you like to play with numbers 1, 2 or **3**?

Each with their own color
that suits them just **fine**,

It's easy to find them.
No need for a **sign!**

The 5's are all red, and
the 3's are bright **pink**.

Onion breath likes the green 7's—
Phew-y now they **stink!**

With playtime at night and children sleeping by **day,**

Gigglyville's full of opposites. The town's just that **way!**

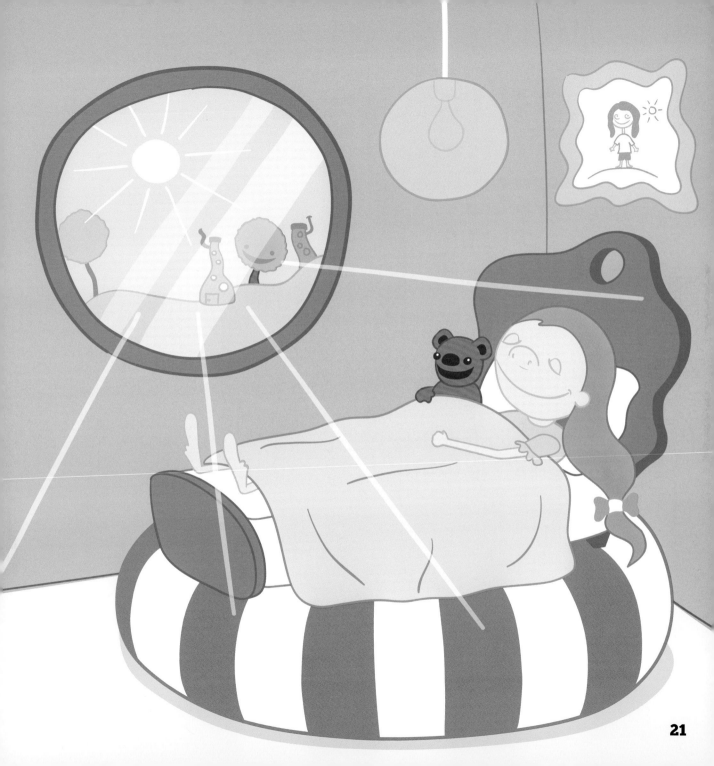

The people walk,
run, skip or hop
wherever they **go**,

And look at their feet they
have one great big **toe**!

They use it for pointing,
for juggling and **hopping**;

And to balance their packages when they go shopping!

They soar through the air on swings hung from the **stars**.
Their houses are splendid, made of bright, odd-shaped **jars**.

24

The windows are circles; each door's shaped like a **square**.
They love to have visitors. Just bring your own **chair!**

Don't forget nothing's ever quite what it **seems**,

Under twinkling stars and shining **moonbeams.**

So wiggle your toes and stay tucked in your warm **bed**,

Remember our Laughmare and all that's been **said**,

Where all you need to bring
is your smiling **face.**

Close your eyes now
and imagine this
magical **place,**

It's a time for adventure,
a place just for **fun**,

Where you will be laughing
'til you see the **sun!**

About the Author

J.E. Laufer

Judy Egett Laufer was born in Budapest, Hungary and immigrated to North America as a young child. The award-winning author of *Where Did Papa Go?*, Laufer spent 10 happy years as a kindergarten teacher and is inspired by the innocence and imagination of children. Judy loves to laugh every day and hopes *Last Night I Had a Laughmare* will send sleepyheads to bed with a smile! Raised primarily in Canada, she now lives in the Southwest with her husband and son.

"Looks like we may have the next Dr. Seuss!

What an imaginative, creative and delightful story. Colorful, zany characters that you won't soon forget. We all know that laughter is the best medicine! This is a terrific bedtime, nap time or anytime story!"

- Dr. Jeffrey L. Derevensky
Professor, School/Applied Child Psychology
Professor, Psychiatry McGill University
Montreal, Quebec

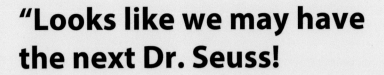

31

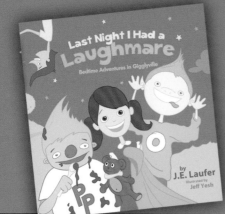

Last Night I Had a Laughmare
Bedtime Adventures in Gigglyville

Clever rhymes and vivid imagery bring Laufer's delightful picture book to life with laugh-out-loud wit and adventure. *Last Night I Had a Laughmare* makes bedtime a magical time for sleepyheads of all ages, taking them on an exciting romp through the land of Gigglyville. The fun doesn't stop until morning!

ITEM	QTY	Unit Price	TOTAL
Last Night I Had a Laughmare (ISBN: 978-1-881669-01-2)		**$16.95 US** **$18.95 CAN**	
➤ ➤ ➤ ➤ ➤ ➤ ➤ ➤ ➤ ➤ ➤ ➤ ➤ ➤ **Subtotal**			
8.8% sales tax – on all orders originating in Arizona. ***Tax**			
\$8.00 or 10% of the total order – whichever is greater. Ground shipping. Allow 1 to 2 weeks for delivery. ***Shipping**			
Mail form to: Little Egg Publishing Company, 1331 N. 7th Street Suite 375, Phoenix, AZ 85006 **TOTAL**			

NAME: _____   ADDRESS: _____

CITY, STATE, ZIP: _____   DAYTIME PHONE: _____

EMAIL: _____   FAX: _____

Method of Payment:
❑VISA ❑MasterCard

▲ account number   ▲ expiration date

▲ signature   ▲ 3 digit security number

Published by

Little Egg Publishing Company
1331 N. 7th Street Suite 375
Phoenix, AZ 85006
(602) 539-5839 fax: (480) 443-8183
www.LittleEggPublishing.com

www.LaughmareBook.com

Book J.E. Laufer or "Purple Pudding" at your next event!
Check website for info!

J.E. Laufer with Snowy